599.88   Goodall, Jane.   6165
GOO
          The chimpanzee
          family book.

                                        $15.20

DATE DUE	BORROWER'S NAME		ROOM NO.
FEB 7 1995			
FEB 2 7 1995			

BIO   Deēgan, P.
THO
       Clarence Thomas

UNITED STATES SUPREME COURT LIBRARY

Clarence Thomas

by Paul J. Deegan

Published by Abdo & Daughters, 6535 Cecilia Circle, Edina, Minnesota 55439.

Copyright © 1992 by Abdo Consulting Group, Inc., Pentagon Tower, P.O. Box 36036, Minneapolis, Minnesota 55435. International copyrights reserved in all counties. No part of this book may be reproduced in any form without written permission from the publisher. Printed in the United States.

Photo credits: A/P Wide World Photos-5
                    Archive Photos-cover
                    UPI/Bettmann-14, 22, 29

Edited by: Bob Italia

Library of Congress Cataloging-in-Publication Data

Deegan, Paul J., 1937-
        Clarence Thomas / written by Paul Deegan ; [edited by Bob Italia].
            p. cm. — (Supreme Court justices)
        Includes index.
        Summary: A career biography of Supreme Court Associate Justice Clarence
    Thomas.
        ISBN 1-56239-088-0
        1. Thomas, Clarence, 1948-   —Juvenile literature. 2. Judges—United States—
    Biography—Juvenile literature. [1. Thomas, Clarence, 1948- . 2. Judges. 3. United
    States. Supreme Court—Biography. 4. Afro-Americans—Biography.] I. Italia, Robert,
    1955- . II. Title. III. Series.
    KF8745.T48D44 1992
    347.73'2634—dc20
    [B]
    [347.3073534]
    [B]
                                                                    92-13717
                                                                        CIP
                                                                         AC

Table of Contents

Against All Odds

He was born in poverty. He was a black in the rural South. When he was two years old, his father left home. When he was seven, he went to live with his grandfather. Life was hard.

"Study hard," said his grandfather. "Learn."

"No one can take your education away from you. You won't be dependent on whites for success."

Clarence Thomas believed his grandfather. As a young man, he left the South to study on the East Coast where he earned a law degree. Years later Clarence Thomas was appointed to the United States Supreme Court.

A high school yearbook photo of Thomas studying at his desk.

Against all odds, the poor black youngster had reached the top. He became only the 106th person in United States history to sit on the Supreme Court. He was the second black associate justice. At age 43, he now was part of the nation's primarily white, usually wealthy power structure.

The journey to the top was not easy. He felt the sting of racial prejudice along the way. Even at the end of the journey, he faced a bitter battle.

From Rural Poverty to National Figure

Clarence Thomas was born in 1948 in a wooden house in the rural Georgia town of Pinpoint. The all-black community had neither paved streets nor sewers. Clarence's mother, Leola Williams, was 18 when he was born. She already had an infant daughter.

When Clarence was two years old, his father left the family. Clarence's mother was pregnant with a third child, who would be a boy. They were living in a one-room building with a dirt floor. Leola went to work at a nearby processing plant where she received a minimal wage. The children's clothes were second-hand from the local Baptist Church. Shoes were a luxury.

When Clarence was seven, his house burned down. Leola moved the family to Savannah, Georgia. She and her daughter lived with an aunt.

She and her daughter lived with an aunt. Carrying everything they owned in shopping bags, Clarence and his younger brother went to live with their grandfather, Myers Anderson. It was the first time Clarence lived in a house with indoor plumbing.

Anderson made a living selling ice and coal from the back of a pickup truck. He was uneducated and was not a good reader. However, he believed strongly in education. He told Clarence that if he prepared himself well, he would be less dependent on the white man. Anderson put the Baptist-born Thomas in nearby St. Benedict the Moor School. The school was staffed by Irish Catholic nuns. The Franciscan Sisters were strict. But Clarence responded well to their demands and earned good grades.

Clarence spent eight years at St. Benedict's. The Sisters convinced him that his keys to success were hard work and determination. He would have to overcome several handicaps — he was a black, fatherless, poor, and a Catholic in the 1950s South.

Grandfather Helps Shape Views

At his grandfather's house, Thomas's future beliefs began to form. Myers Anderson disliked people he thought depended upon government welfare programs. Anderson thought these people should try to make their way on their own. He, himself, had made his way without help. "Man hasn't got no business on relief as long as he can work," Anderson told Clarence. Despite this viewpoint, Anderson was a strong Democrat. He also was an active member of the National Association for the Advancement of Colored People (NAACP). The NAACP is a pioneer civil rights organization. Anderson took Clarence to the local NAACP chapter meetings.

Myers Anderson also was a devout Catholic. So when Clarence was high school age, he attended St. John Vianney Minor Seminary in Savannah. He quarterbacked the school's football team. St. John's was a boarding school. One night, when lights were out in the dorm, another student teased Clarence. "Smile, Clarence," he said, "so we can see you." When he graduated in 1967, Clarence was the only black in his class.

Clarence then left Georgia to attend Immaculate Conception Seminary in Conception, a northwest Missouri town. A college-level seminary was the next step in studies for the priesthood. Clarence spent eight months in Conception before deciding he did not want to be a priest. Thomas also experienced discrimination at the Missouri school.

Thomas moved from the South after leaving the seminary. He transferred to Holy Cross College, a Jesuit school in Worcester, Massachusetts, west of Boston. He graduated from Holy Cross with a major in English. The school's president said in 1991 that the change had to have been difficult for Thomas. Thomas was "coming up as a black from the South into a northeastern white community,..." Father John Brooks, S.J. said, "But he didn't let it throw him at all."

Thomas was not yet a staunch conservative. At Holy Cross he was a founding member of the Black Student Union and looked with favor upon the Black Panthers, a racial organization. He ended his letters with the slogan, "Power to the people."

The difference in his views then and later were noted when he became front page news some 20 years later. Thomas became known for opposing government efforts to deal with racial prejudice. *Time* magazine noted that Thomas had benefited from such efforts.

For example, Thomas got into law school under a program favoring minorities – an affirmative action program. Thomas went to law school at Yale University after graduating from Holy Cross. The Yale campus is in New Haven, Connecticut, on Long Island Sound, not far from New York City. Thomas graduated from Law School in 1973 and went back to Missouri.

Danforth Connection Formed

Thomas's first job as a lawyer was in the Missouri Attorney General's office in Jefferson City. Thomas was the only black working for Attorney General John Danforth. Thomas worked on felony appeals, on tax cases and for the state's Human Rights Commission. In the later role, he handled job discrimination items. Thomas was "a compassionate kind of conservative," Danforth said. He was "not rigid…in his views."

Thomas left Danforth's office to work as a corporate lawyer for the Monsanto company from 1977 to 1979. When Danforth became a United States Senator, Thomas returned to work for him as a legislative assistant. Then Thomas briefly served in the United States Department of Education's civil rights division.

Thomas Heads Federal Commission

President Ronald Reagan took office in 1980. In 1982 Thomas was named chairman of the five-member Equal Employment Opportunity Commission (EEOC). Once Thomas said he felt "insulted" about being named to this position. He meant that because he was black, it was assumed he would be good in a civil rights job. He preferred a job in the Reagan administration using his knowledge of taxation and corporate law.

Thomas stayed in the EEOC position for almost eight years. He was still there when George Bush became President in 1989. His stay was controversial.

Liberal Democrats and civil rights groups said Thomas failed to aggressively enforce anti-discrimination laws. Thomas's supporters said he moved a troubled agency into a well-run organization. They said the EEOC helped real discrimination victims.

During his years on the EEOC, Thomas's dislike for affirmative action was strengthened. He did not hide his opposition to the use of racial preferences. In a 1985 law review article, he wrote:

"There is an enormous amount of rhetoric (extravagant language) these days on both sides of the civil rights issue...I am tired of the rhetoric – the rhetoric about quotas and about affirmative action. It is a supreme waste of time. It precludes (prevents) more positive and enlightened discussion, and it is no longer relevant."

Clarence Thomas, chairman of the Equal Employment Opportunity Commission, 1985.

Thomas wrote in 1987 that affirmative action programs "create a narcotic of dependency, not an ethic of responsibility and independence. They are at best an irrelevance, covering up some real problems..." Thomas also said affirmative action was "social engineering."

In 1990 President Bush named Thomas to the United States Court of Appeals for the District of Columbia Circuit. Several previous Supreme Court justices had served on this Washington, D.C., appellate court. Eighteen months after Thomas became an appellate court judge, Thurgood Marshall resigned from the Supreme Court. Associate Justice Marshall was the only black ever to serve on the high court.

President Ponders Choices

Associate Justice Marshall made his decision known on June 27, 1991. The Supreme Court had just recessed for the summer. Although Marshall was 82 years old, his resignation came as a surprise in Washington, D.C. Marshall had been a justice for 24 years. He had said the Supreme Court was a "lifetime term" and that he would never retire. His health seemed good.

Marshall's decision to step down was seen as a sign of his growing anger and discouragement. A solid conservative majority was reshaping the viewpoint of the Supreme Court.

Marshall's resignation meant President Bush had to appoint a successor. The President faced pressure to continue moving the Court down a conservative path. There also was pressure to appoint another black justice.

President Bush was in the midst of a bitter battle with civil rights groups, Democrats, and moderate Republicans. The issue was quotas in a civil rights bill Congress was considering.

Therefore, it was thought, the President would be eager to send a message of friendship to blacks.

The President considered a list of choices. Clarence Thomas was on the list. White House advisers said President Bush wanted to appoint a member of a minority. Bush was impressed by Thomas's "good record." The President also liked Thomas. However, advisers said, "all things being equal," the President preferred an Hispanic man from Bush's adopted state of Texas.

Emilio Garza, 43, was a new member of the Fifth U.S. Circuit Court of Appeals in San Antonio. Garza was brought to Washington for an interview with Justice Department officials. But senior advisers told Bush that Garza was "not ready" for an appointment to the high court. For instance, Garza had yet to write an opinion on the appellate court.

So the President chose the 43-year-old Thomas to be an associate justice of the United States Supreme Court.

The President Reveals His Choice

resident Bush announced his choice on July 1, 1991. He presented Clarence Thomas to the public at the Bush vacation residence in Kennebunkport, Maine.

A newspaper headline said: "Bush nominates racial-quota foe to Marshall seat." Thomas stood in stark contrast to Justice Marshall. The retiring justice had been one of the nation's best civil rights lawyers before his appointment to the Court. Marshall was a staunch member of the Court's liberal faction. Thomas, half Marshall's age, was opposed to all racial preferences. Thomas, a newspaper said, had "risen in Republican ranks as an advocate of bootstrap conservatism."

President Bush had found a black who was in tune with Republican beliefs. Minorities don't need affirmative action to succeed. What is important is to remove discrimination.

President Bush was nominating a black to replace a black justice. But the President said he did not "feel he (Thomas) is a quota."

"I expressed my respect for the ground that Mr. Justice Marshall plowed, but I don't feel there should be a black seat on the court or an ethnic seat on the court," the President said.

He said he nominated Thomas because he was "the best man" for the job.

Many critics of the appointment questioned the President's sincerity in making this statement. A political analyst said on July 3, "Forget the President's denials." The nomination of Thomas had nothing to do with the law. It had "almost everything to do with the raw politics of race."

A Harvard Law School professor said Thomas was "certainly qualified." But said Christopher Edley Jr., "No one can look at (his) record and find the claim he was the best qualified person" at all believable. A *Time* magazine report said that "As Supreme Court nominees go, Thomas has little judicial experience. He is not a brilliant legal scholar, a weighty thinker or even the author of numerous opinions."

Thomas's supporters said the Supreme Court was dominated by people with "privileged upbringings." They said Thomas, as Marshall had done, would bring a different perspective. A former law school classmate said Thomas understood "what it's like to be black and poor in this country and to face the worst kinds of prejudice."

A friend said Thomas got the nomination "strictly on the merits." He said Thomas resented "the notion that he's ever gotten anywhere because he's black." Thomas had addressed that question himself at Kennebunkport. A reporter had asked him what he would say to critics who said he was selected only because he was black and not because he had "worked to advance the cause of blacks."

Thomas had replied: "I think a lot worse things have been said. I disagree with that, but I'll have to live with it."

Only in America

President Bush presented Thomas to the public on July 1 as a man whose life was an inspiration. Thomas was offered as proof that someone can overcome unfavorable beginnings without special favors.

"If credit accrues to him for coming up through a tough life as a minority in this country, so much the better," the President said. "It proves he can do it, get the job done. And so that does nothing but enhance the Court, in my view."

Clarence Thomas said in Kennebunkport: "In my view, only in America could this have been possible." Standing alongside the President, Thomas told reporters, "As a child I could not dare dream that I would ever see the Supreme Court, not to mention be nominated to it."

President Bush introduces Judge Thomas as a nominee to fill the vacancy on the Supreme Court created by the retirement of Justice Thurgood Marshall, July 1, 1991.

23

Thomas also thanked "all of those who helped me along the way to this moment in my life." He singled out his grandparents, his mother, and "the nuns." The latter was a reference to his teachers at St. Benedict's in Savannah. All of these people, he said, stressed to him the importance of "growing up to make something of myself."

Thomas's Struggle Begins

The United States Constitution requires the Senate's "advice and consent" on a Supreme Court appointment. White House aides expected a fight over Thomas's confirmation. Before his nomination, Thomas had promised President Bush that he "would stick out the confirmation process no matter how tough it got." Little did anyone know how tough it would be. The confirmation process would become harsh and ugly.

Administration officials knew Thomas's nomination would be attacked by most Democrats and by civil rights activists. Some Thomas opponents accused President Bush of making a cynical choice. He had picked a black, and blacks probably would hesitate to object to his choice. Yet, most blacks opposed Thomas's conservative positions. Most Senators would find it difficult to vote against a black nominee who had been disadvantaged – most Senators had been neither.

25

The Bush administration decided there was a way to reduce opponents' criticism. They would portray Thomas as a champion of the poor and oppressed. Thomas had spoken to that image when he faced the press at Kennebunkport. He hoped, he said, to be "an example to those who are where I was and to show them that, indeed, there is hope."

Danforth, the Missouri Republican senator and Thomas's former employer, would be the point man for Thomas in the confirmation process. Danforth had said Thomas's "every motive is that he empathizes with ordinary people; he's one of them. Clarence Thomas has the common touch. In a very real way, he'll be the people's justice."

Thomas Faces the Senate Committee

Thomas's confirmation hearings before the Senate Judiciary Committee were set for September 10, 1991. Eight of the 14 committee members were Democrats. They were sure to seek Thomas's opinions on a variety of subjects. Thomas's recent record did not give them much to review. When nominated three months earlier, Thomas had refused to answer reporters' questions about various topics including abortion. Neither did Senators have much to go on from Thomas's 18 months on the appellate court. He had taken part in only 27 decisions, all of them routine.

Thomas was well prepared to go before the Senate Judiciary Committee. He had spent weeks with White House public relations advisers preparing for the hearings. The administration knew that the 14 committee members would be interested in Thomas's views on a variety of subjects. Thomas began his testimony before the committee by talking about his life.

He recalled his rise from extreme poverty to his position on the District Columbia appeals court. The nominee told the Senators that "No judge worth his or her salt will prejudge a case." Thomas also disassociated himself from many of his past comments.

Some committee members were astonished when he said that he had never discussed *Roe vs. Wade* in private. This was the Supreme Court's 1973 landmark decision on abortion.

Clarence Thomas takes the oath before giving his testimony to the United States Senate Judiciary Committee.

The nine days of Judiciary Committee hearings ended on September 20. During the last four days, Senators heard from interest groups for and against Thomas's confirmation. When the hearings ended, observers thought the committee would vote to approve the confirmation. It was expected that Thomas could join the Supreme Court when it began a new term on October 7.

However, when the vote came on September 27, the committee deadlocked, the vote was 7-7. Never before had the committee come up with a tie vote on a Court nominee. The vote placed the Senate in a unique situation. Previous Judiciary Committees had voted against Court nominations. Twelve times the entire Senate had followed suit. This time the Senate had no recommendation to follow.

The Senate vote was scheduled for October 8, a few days later than had been expected. This meant that the Supreme Court would begin their term with only eight members.

Controversy Delays Vote

Suddenly, however, the confirmation process began to unravel. The Federal Bureau of Investigation (FBI) always does background checks on major federal appointees. The FBI reported the information they gathered on Thomas to the Judiciary Committee. In early October, someone leaked information from the FBI report to the media. The information said a former Thomas aide had charged him with sexual harassment.

When this charge became public, the Senate delayed the confirmation vote. The Senate directed the Judiciary Committee to hold public hearings regarding the charge. Senator Joseph Biden, a Delaware Democrat, was the committee's chairman. Biden said "The nominee has the right to be confronted by his accuser."

The confirmation process was about to get ugly.

The public hearings began on the morning of Friday, October 11, and ended at 1 a.m. on Monday morning. The three days were an ordeal for both the accused and the accuser. It was not one of the U.S. Senate's better moments, either, and the confirmation process itself was tarnished.

The accusation of sexual harassment had been made by Anita Hill. She was a 35-year-old black legal professor at the University of Oklahoma in Norman. While Hill worked in the Department of Education in 1981 and 1982 and at the EEOC from 1982 to 1983, Thomas had been her supervisor. Millions saw and heard on television her claim that Thomas had sexually harassed her while she worked for him. The testimony on both sides included sexual terms seldom spoken in the sedate Senate Caucus Room where the hearings took place.

During two days as a witness, Thomas denied Hill's charges of sexual advancements. "I categorically deny all of the allegations and deny that I ever attempted to date Anita Hill," Thomas told the all-male committee. He also said he was being subjected to "a high-tech lynching for uppity blacks" and said he "would have preferred an assassin's bullet." Hill's truthfulness, character, and even her sanity were questioned by Republican Senators. "In the end, of course," said one reporter, "there would be no winners, only scars."

Even those who heard all the testimony were left wondering what actually happened. The hours of testimony boiled down to who was lying – the man seeking a post on the Supreme Court or the previously unknown law professor?

The question was never resolved. The Senate told the Judiciary Committee not to vote on the issue. The committee was also forbidden to do anything else which might indicate which of the two principals was telling the truth.

Senate Margin Slim

A nomination went back before the entire Senate. On October 15, Senators engaged in a day-long debate before voting whether or not to confirm Thomas. President Bush pressured Senators who hadn't revealed their position. Finally, that night, the vote came.

Clarence Thomas became a Supreme Court associate justice by the narrowest of margins. The 52-48 vote was the lowest margin this century. Eleven Democrats joined 43 Republicans in voting for Thomas. Seven of these Democrats were from the South and were, in many cases, dependent on black votes for re-election.

Thomas would have lost the vote if three more Democrats had voted against his confirmation.

It had been 107 days since President Bush had presented Thomas to the public at Kennebunkport. It probably seemed like 107 years to the new justice. After the vote, Thomas talked to the press outside his Alexandria, Virginia, home. As for the fierce battle over his nomination, he said, "We have to put these things behind us and go forward. This is a time for healing, not a time for anger or...animosity."

But during his two days on the witness stand before the Judiciary Committee, Thomas had railed at those he said wanted to "destroy" him. He said Democratic Senators, liberal interest groups, and the press together "put me and my family through...this kind of living hell." Thus, one reporter asked: "Can Thomas now put behind him the rage and pain of the past 10 days and act as an impartial jurist on cases involving those same groups?"

The Private Side of Clarence Thomas

Thomas is married to
Virginia Lamp Thomas. Virginia works for the
United States Department of Labor as deputy
assistant secretary. Clarence and Ginni Lamp
met in the spring of 1986 and were married by
the following summer. Virginia works in the
department's legislative affairs office.
Described as a "brainy Omaha (Nebraska)
lawyer," Virginia is the one person Clarence
Thomas depends on for advice, a longtime
friend said. He "really listens to (her)."

Clarence Thomas favors a color-blind
society. But some blacks have criticized
Thomas for abandoning his roots because
Virginia Lamp is white. (Thomas was divorced
in 1984 from Kate Ambush, who is black.)
Thomas "marrying a white woman is a sign of
his rejection of the black community," said
Russel Adams. He is chairman of the Afro-
American studies department at mostly-black
Howard University in Washington, D.C.

Clarence, Virginia, and Jamal Thomas live in the Washington suburb of Alexandria. Jamal is Thomas's son from his first marriage. Thomas and his wife enjoy morning runs together and sometimes drive to work together in Thomas's black Corvette. Clarence and Virginia attend the Truro Episcopal Church, a charismatic congregation.

Leona Williams, Thomas's mother, now lives in Savannah, Georgia. She works as a receptionist and nurse's aid at a hospital. His grandfather, Myers Anderson, died in 1983.

What Did Myers Anderson Know?

Still a young man, Justice Thomas could sit on the Supreme Court for decades. His reputation in his brief time as a judge was favorable. What he will do as a Supreme Court associate justice remains to be seen. Whatever decisions he faces, they probably will never be as difficult as his confirmation hearing.

Whatever mark he makes on the Supreme Court, Clarence Thomas's life represents the American dream. He has risen from a dirt floor beginning in a segregated town to the height of power.

Clarence Thomas once thought that his grandfather's hopes for him were beyond reach. Today he sits on the nation's highest court. Maybe Myers Anderson knew something nobody else did!

Glossary

Affirmative Action: An active effort to improve the employment or educational opportunities of members of minority groups and women.

Associate Justice: A member of the Supreme Court.

Attorney General: The chief law officer of a nation or state who represents the government in litigation and serves as its principal legal adviser.

Black Panthers: An organization of militant American blacks.

Civil Rights: The rights of personal liberty guaranteed to U.S. citizens by the 13th and the 14th amendments to the Constitution.

Congress: The lawmaking body of the United States of America.

Conservative: Inclined to keep things as they are or were in the past.

Poverty: The state of one who lacks a usual or socially acceptable amount of money or material possessions.

Prejudice: An opinion formed against a person without taking time and care to judge fairly.

United States Court of Appeals: A court hearing appeals from the decisions of lower courts. something nobody else did!

Index